PEANUTS®

Snoopy's Christmas
SURPRISE

Based on the comic strip PEANUTS by
Charles M. Schulz
Written by Jason Cooper
Illustrated by Vicki Scott

SIMON SPOTLIGHT
An imprint of Simon & Schuster Children's Publishing Division
New York   London   Toronto   Sydney   New Delhi
1230 Avenue of the Americas, New York, New York 10020
This Simon Spotlight paperback edition September 2018
© 2018 Peanuts Worldwide LLC
For information about special discounts for bulk purchases, please contact Simon & Schuster Special Sales at
1-866-506-1949 or business@simonandschuster.com.
Manufactured in the United States of America 0818 LAK
2 4 6 8 10 9 7 5 3 1
ISBN 978-1-5344-2181-3
ISBN 978-1-5344-2182-0 (eBook)

D1122335

Snoopy really enjoys the holiday season. He likes the decorations and the songs, and he *loves* receiving Christmas cards! This year he got a postcard from his brother Spike.

Snoopy excitedly shows the card to Charlie Brown.
"Boy, wouldn't it be fun to see Spike this Christmas?" Charlie Brown asks.
Snoopy agrees that it would be fun!

Snoopy writes a letter to Spike, inviting him to his home.

DEAR SPIKE,

WHY NOT LEAVE THE DESERT THIS HOLIDAY SEASON
AND SPEND CHRISTMAS WITH ME?

IT WOULD BE FUN!

HO, HO, HO!
SNOOPY

Snoopy can't wait for Spike's visit! He cleans his guest room and buys more root beer. But he receives sad news in Spike's response:

DEAR SNOOPY,

I'M SORRY, BUT I CAN'T AFFORD TO COME SEE YOU THIS YEAR.
I HOPE WE'LL BE ABLE TO GET TOGETHER SOME OTHER TIME.

MERRY CHRISTMAS!

LOVE,
SPIKE

Snoopy is devastated.

"I'm sorry, Snoopy," Charlie Brown says. "I wish I could give you bus fare for Spike, but I don't have much money, either."

Snoopy sighs and walks back to his doghouse.

"We'll have a nice Christmas anyway," Charlie Brown promises.

As Christmas inches closer, almost everyone gets excited. Snoopy, though, has a bad case of the holiday blues. Not even his bird best friend, Woodstock, can cheer him up. Usually a batch of Woodstock's homemade Christmas cookies makes Snoopy feel better. But not this time. Snoopy still feels sad.

What can I do to get Snoopy into the Christmas spirit? Charlie Brown wonders. He decides to ask his friend Lucy. She is always ready to give advice—provided you have a nickel.

Lucy reads the letter from Spike. "Snoopy misses his family," she says. "How sad."

"I know," Charlie Brown agrees. "Can you imagine not seeing your brothers during the holidays?"

"Yes!" Lucy says. "But I'd miss the presents they give me."

"What do you think I should do, Lucy?" Charlie Brown asks.

"Try being extra nice to Snoopy, and let his friends know how he's feeling, too," Lucy advises. "He'll learn that even though he can't see his family, he's loved and appreciated by his friends here."

Charlie Brown thanks Lucy for her help and starts thinking up ideas to make his beagle feel better.

Snoopy's pal Peppermint Patty knits him a Christmas sweater. Snoopy tries it on. He looks like a sheep!

Peppermint Patty thinks he looks great. "He looks pretty good, doesn't he, Chuck?"

Schroeder drops by with his piano to play some holiday music for Snoopy. But the sweet music makes him miss Spike even more. Snoopy howls loudly and Schroeder gets the hint.

"Everyone's a critic," says Schroeder.

Later that day, Lucy hands Charlie Brown an invitation to her Christmas party. "Now remember, come late and help me clean up," she reminds him. "By the way, how's Snoopy?"

"He's still sad," Charlie Brown says. "I've tried everything, but I don't know how to make him happy."

Lucy is quiet for a moment, then she smiles. "I think there's only one thing to do."

Before Charlie Brown can ask her what it is, Lucy runs off.

The next day, Lucy visits Snoopy. "Ohhh, Snoopy! I've got a surprise for you!" she says.

Snoopy turns around to see Lucy . . . and Spike! The dogs jump for joy and give each other a big hug.

Charlie Brown is surprised as well. "Lucy! This is wonderful! How did this happen?" he asks.

"I've been saving my nickels all year to buy myself something nice," Lucy says. "But I realized, at Christmas, I should do something nice for someone else."

Snoopy and Spike give Lucy a big hug too. She smiles and blushes. "Merry Christmas, Snoopy!"